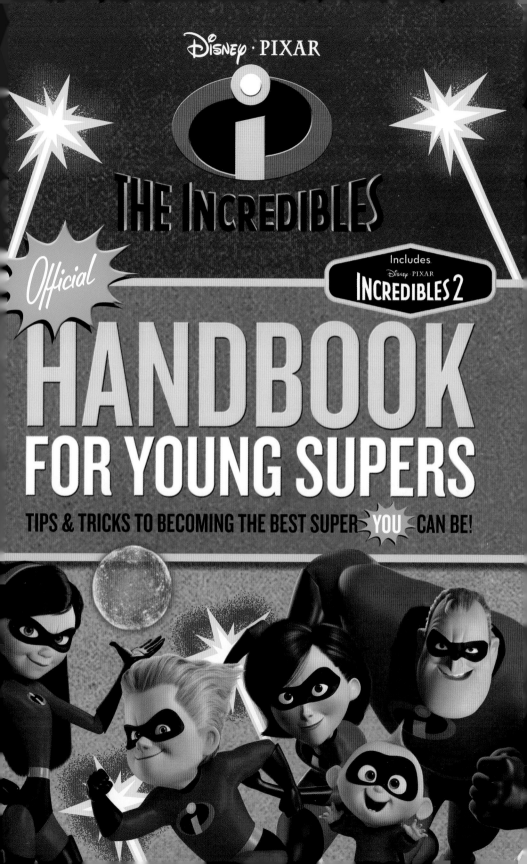

SAVING THE DAY ONE DAY AT A TIME

DISCOVER ALL THE INS AND OUTS OF FIGHTING CRIME, SUPER TRAINING, BECOMING PART OF A SUPER TEAM AND MORE WITH THIS OFFICIAL GUIDE TO BEING A SUPER! IT'S THE BEST HANDBOOK A HERO-IN-TRAINING COULD ASK FOR.

YOU'RE NOT GOOD, YOU'RE SUPER!

CONTENTS

PLUS

DEFINING YOUR SUPER PERSONA

DETERMINE WHAT KINDS OF SUPER POWERS YOU HAVE, WHAT YOUR SUPERSUIT WILL LOOK LIKE AND ALL THE OTHER ESSENTIALS YOU NEED TO BE A SUPER.

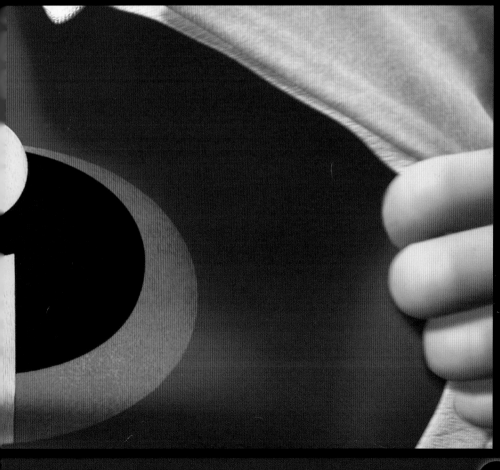

DISCOVER YOUR POWERS!

SUPERS HAVE ALL KINDS OF AMAZING, UNEXPECTED POWERS. SOME ARE BORN WITH THEM, AND OTHERS GAIN THEM THROUGH RANDOM ACCIDENTS, EXPERIMENTS OR STROKES OF LUCK. AS YOU GET OLDER, YOU MIGHT EVEN DISCOVER YOU HAVE ABILITIES YOU NEVER KNEW YOU POSSESSED!

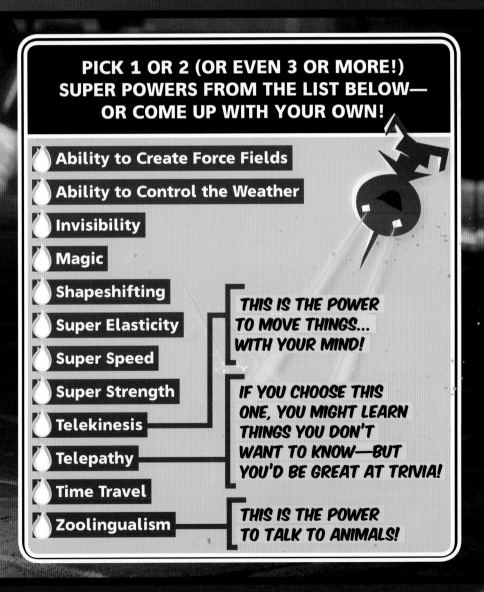

PICK 1 OR 2 (OR EVEN 3 OR MORE!) SUPER POWERS FROM THE LIST BELOW— OR COME UP WITH YOUR OWN!

- Ability to Create Force Fields
- Ability to Control the Weather
- Invisibility
- Magic
- Shapeshifting
- Super Elasticity
- Super Speed
- Super Strength
- Telekinesis
- Telepathy
- Time Travel
- Zoolingualism

THIS IS THE POWER TO MOVE THINGS... WITH YOUR MIND!

IF YOU CHOOSE THIS ONE, YOU MIGHT LEARN THINGS YOU DON'T WANT TO KNOW—BUT YOU'D BE GREAT AT TRIVIA!

THIS IS THE POWER TO TALK TO ANIMALS!

DETERMINE YOUR ORIGIN

IF YOU'RE GOING TO BE A SUPER, YOU'LL NEED AN ORIGIN STORY THAT EXPLAINS HOW YOU GOT YOUR POWERS AND WHAT MADE YOU DECIDE TO USE THEM FOR GOOD.

"WE WANNA FIG BAD GUYS! IT DEFINES WHO AM."

Did you fall in a radioactive pit? Were you born into a Super family, like Violet, Dash and Jack-Jack? Did a sorcerer or a magician give you powers? The possibilities are endless!

You also might want to consider crafting an origin story that connects with your powers. For example, if you can run extraordinarily fast, maybe your DNA somehow got spliced with a cheetah's.

Once you've determined how you got your powers, think about what made you decide to use them to fight crime. Perhaps someone was mean to you or someone you know, or you were raised to always stand up for those who can't stand up for themselves.

REMEMBER, BEING A SUPER ISN'T ALWAYS EASY. WHEN THINGS GET A LITTLE ROUGH AND YOU FEEL LIKE GIVING UP, REMINDING YOURSELF OF YOUR ORIGIN STORY WILL GIVE YOU THE STRENGTH TO KEEP ON GOING!

DECIDE YOUR ALTER EGO

UNFORTUNATELY, IT'S NOT SAFE TO LET EVERYONE KNOW THAT YOU'RE A SUPER (AND TRUTH BE TOLD, THE PAY'S NOT GREAT). SO START FIGURING OUT WHAT ELSE YOU WANT TO BE WHEN YOU GROW UP!

PICK A JOB FROM BELOW, OR COME UP WITH YOUR OWN!

Detective

Pro You'll get lots of leads on criminals to catch in the act!

Con Your detective partner might figure out your secret.

Fashion Designer

Pro You'd be great at mending your own supersuit—or even redesigning it!

Con You'd have Edna Mode as your competition!

Doctor

Pro It would be handy to know how to patch yourself up.

Con Doctors work pretty long hours—you might no have time to fight crime.

WHATEVER YOU PICK, MAKE SURE YOU LIKE DOING IT... AND THAT YOUR BOSS LIKES YOU!

Journalist

Pro You'll know if the media is getting close to figuring out your identity.

Con You'll have a hard time fighting villains if you're supposed to be reporting about them!

Pilot

Pro Knowing how to fly a plane could be useful!

Con You can't exactly leave during your shift if there's a Super emergency.

Garbage Collector

Pro You'll know every alley in your city like the back of your hand.

Con You'll probably get pretty smelly!

SUPER ATTIRE 101

YOUR SUPER ATTIRE SHOULD ACCOMPLISH THREE MAIN GOALS:

1. PROTECT YOUR IDENTITY.

2. IDENTIFY YOURSELF AS A SUPER TO WOULD-BE CRIMINALS AND THE AUTHORITIES— NOT TO MENTION YOUR ADORING PUBLIC.

3. FACILITATE EASE OF MOVEMENT AND USE OF YOUR POWERS.

SUPER FASHION DOS AND DON'TS

Dos

✔ Breathable/ inflammable/ stretchy material

✔ Sleek lines

✔ Bold graphics

Don'ts

✘ Capes

✘ Clashing colors

✘ Masks that obscure your vision

DESIGN YOUR SUPERSUIT!

Now that you know everything about supersuits, it's time to design your own!

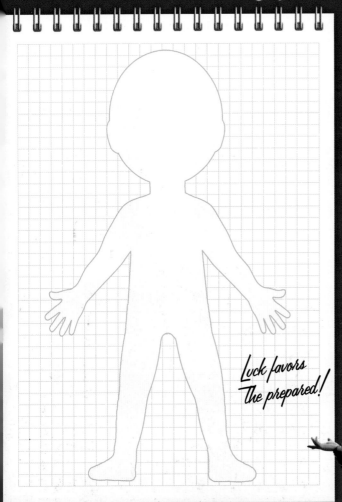

Luck favors the prepared!

Think about designing a special symbol for yourself, or determine if your suit needs anything special based on your powers. For example, Violet's supersuit turns invisible when she does, and Elastigirl's supersuit is as stretchy as she is. What will your suit need to do?

WE CAN'T STRESS IT ENOUGH—
NO CAPES!!!

THUNDERHEAD
ALL WAS WELL. ANOTHER DAY SAVED, WHEN...HIS CAPE SNAGGED ON A MISSILE FIN!

STRATOGALE

CAPE CAUGHT IN A JET TURBINE!

META MAN

EXPRESS ELEVATOR!

DEFINING YOUR SUPER PERSONA

SNAGGED ON TAKEOFF!

DYNAGUY

SPLASHDOWN

SUCKED INTO A VORTEX!

NO CAPES!!!

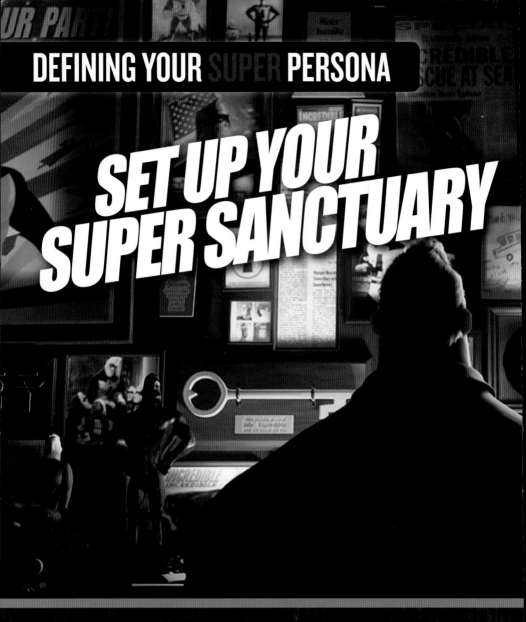

SET UP YOUR SUPER SANCTUARY

POTENTIAL SANCTUARY SPOTS

If there aren't any good caves or abandoned fortresses nearby, consider one of these places for your hideaway. They might not be flashy, but on the plus side, no one will ever suspect such common locales are actually areas where Supers are hanging out!

EVERY SUPER NEEDS A PLACE OF HIS OR HER OWN. SUPER SANCTUARIES ARE THE IDEAL PLACE FOR PLANNING, TRAINING, BROODING OR EVEN HAVING OVER SOME SUPER FRIENDS!

THINK ABOUT WHERE YOUR SUPER SANCTUARY WOULD BE. IS ITS LOCATION RELATED TO YOUR POWERS IN SOME WAY?

Here are some more things to consider when choosing your hideaway:

- Is it difficult for others to find?
- Can you get to the sanctuary quickly?
- Does it have enough space to store your Super things?

TREE FORT

CLOSET

GARAGE

BASEMENT

REFUGE RENOVATION

JUST LIKE ANYTHING ELSE, WHEN IT COMES TO YOUR SANCTUARY, IT'S WHAT'S ON THE INSIDE THAT COUNTS! STOCK YOUR HIDEAWAY WITH EVERYTHING YOU'LL NEED, SUCH AS:

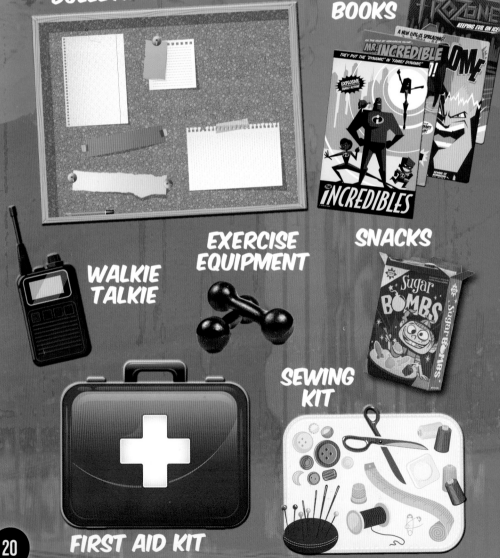

BULLETIN BOARD

COMIC BOOKS

WALKIE TALKIE

EXERCISE EQUIPMENT

SNACKS

SEWING KIT

FIRST AID KIT

DESIGN YOUR SANCTUARY

PLAN OUT WHAT YOUR SANCTUARY WILL LOOK LIKE! CREATE YOUR OWN FLOOR PLAN ON THE GRAPH PAPER BELOW.

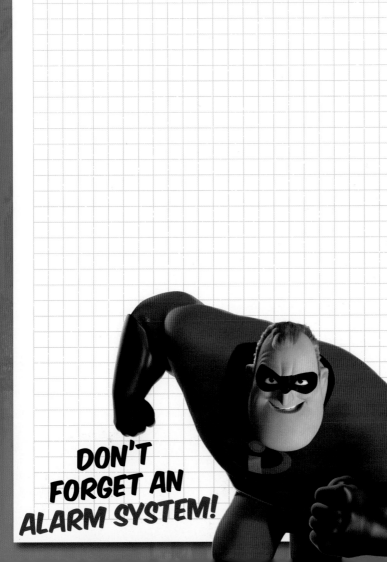

DON'T FORGET AN ALARM SYSTEM!

THE IMPORTANCE OF A MORAL CODE

As a Super you have incredible powers, and it's your duty to use them to help the world. At the same time, nobody's perfect— you'll make mistakes—and it's impossible to help everyone. That's why it's good to have a moral code. If you always follow it, you'll know you're doing a good job.

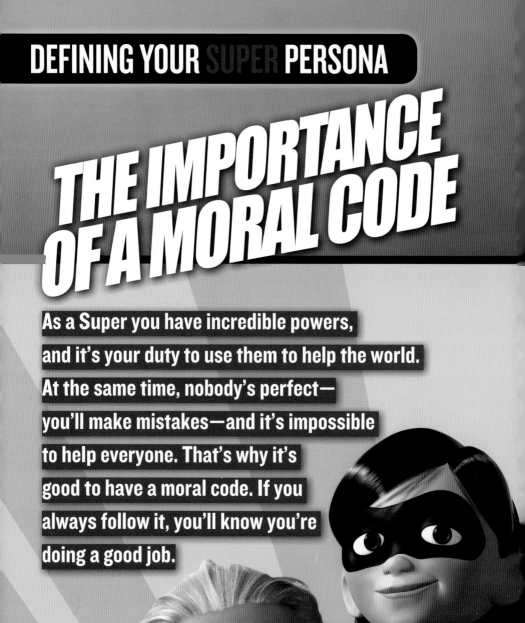

ASPECTS OF YOUR MORAL CODE CAN INCLUDE THINGS LIKE:

- **ALWAYS CHOOSE TO DO GOOD.**
- **ALWAYS MAKE TIME TO BE POLITE.**
- **BE GRATEFUL TO YOUR FANS AND ADMIRERS.**
- **MAKE TIME FOR YOUR FAMILY.**

WRITE OUT YOUR OWN MORAL CODE THAT YOU PROMISE TO FOLLOW.

I, _____,
promise to uphold my duties as a Super.
I promise to always

_____

_____

_____

_____

_____
Signature

23

THE ART OF THE SUPER QUIP

SUPERS DON'T JUST USE THEIR POWERS TO FIGHT CRIME—THEY USE THEIR WITS, TOO! ONE OF THE BEST WAYS TO FLEX YOUR MENTAL MUSCLE IS BY LANDING THE PERFECT PUN. PUNS OFTEN RELY ON SIMILAR SOUNDING WORDS, OR WORDS WITH DOUBLE MEANINGS. FOR EXAMPLE, IF YOU JUST DISABLED THE LEFT SIDE OF A ROBOT, YOU COULD SAY, "DON'T WORRY—YOU'RE ALL RIGHT!"

MAKING PUNS REQUIRES SOME FLEXIBILITY!

To ensure your puns are as powerful as your punches, try these tricks!

1. **Rhyme in your head while speaking with someone.** If you can come up with a good homophone (a word that sounds like another word), that might be fodder for a pun. For example, if you're looking at a large pile of hats, you might be thinking bats, rats, cats...and then you can say "Looks like someone let the hat out of the bag!"

2. **Timing is everything.** Your pun should have to do with whatever's happening at the moment. So if you're in the midst of fighting a villain who uses magnets, you might say something about how their suit is "repelling."

3. **Increase your vocabulary.** The more words you know, the more you'll have at your disposal when making a pun! Whenever you hear a word you don't know, write it down and look it up. You can also increase your vocabulary by reading new books.

WHAT'S A SUPER'S FAVORITE PART OF A JOKE?

THE PUNCH LINE!

DETERMINE YOUR SECRET IDENTITY'S ATTITUDE

THOUGH ALL SUPERS CHOOSE TO BE GOOD, YOU CAN STILL HAVE YOUR OWN PERSONALITY. YOUR ATTITUDE MIGHT AFFECT WHAT ROLE YOU PLAY IN A SUPER TEAM (READ MORE ABOUT THAT IN THE NEXT CHAPTER!), HELP YOU DECIDE WHAT YOUR SUIT LOOKS LIKE (MAYBE DON'T GO WITH POLKA DOTS IF YOU ARE VERY SERIOUS) AND MAY EVEN DETERMINE WHAT KINDS OF ADMIRERS YOU'LL HAVE.

DASH WOULD DEFINITELY HAVE LEGIONS OF ADMIRERS—BUT THEY HAVE TO BE QUICK ENOUGH TO SEE HIM!

ANSWER THE QUESTIONS BELOW TO FIGURE OUT YOUR SUPER PERSONA!

I. Do you like to make quips?

A. I love to!

B. No, crime fighting is serious work.

C. Eh, if I can think of one.

2. Do you enjoy working with a team?

A. Of course—there's more people to laugh at my jokes!

B. I work alone. Always.

C. Maybe. I can get by on my own, but I can't drive.

3. Do you want citizens to admire you?

A. They already do!

B. No, I am their silent, invisible savior.

C. They don't have to, but it's nice to be appreciated.

4. Would you give a speech to schoolchildren?

A. I'd give a speech to anyone who will listen!

B. Absolutely not. Speeches are my only weakness.

C. Sure, those kids should learn how to stay safe!

5. Do you consider yourself a beacon of light?

A. Of course! No one shines brighter than me!

B. No—I only fight in the shadows.

C. I try to be!

Mostly As
You're one hilarious Super! Just make sure you're taking enough time in between cracking jokes to do some good.

Mostly Bs
You're a dark, mysterious, sort of Super. But remember to remind yourself that it's OK to come out of the shadows sometimes.

Mostly Cs
You're a classically brave and heroic Super! You understand that the best thing about your abilities is that you have the ability to help.

MEET MR. INCREDIBLE

NAME: ROBERT (BOB) PARR

POWERS MEGA STRENGTH, NEAR INVULNERABILITY

HEIGHT 6'8"

HAIR BLONDE

AGE 40s

WEIGHT 348 LBS

SUPERSUIT DESIGNER EDNA MODE

KNOWN ASSOCIATES ELASTIGIRL, FROZONE

CHILDREN VIOLET, DASH, JACK-JACK

TRIVIA WON LEGENDARY EATING CONTEST
WITH THUNDERHEAD AT NSA PICNIC, EATING
47 BOYSENBERRY PIES,
8 BANANA CREAMS, 3 APPLE-CRUMBS
AND A LITER OF MAYONNAISE.

STRENGTH

ENDURANCE

INTELLIGENCE

AGILITY

INDESTRUCTIBILITY

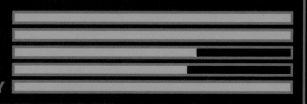

- Mr. Incredible's nickname around the National Supers Agency (NSA) used to be "Mr. Inedible."

- He can be easily distracted and has an inability to set priorities.

- The NSA had supplied him with the Incredibile, a special car with onboard weaponry, danger finder and evasion countermeasures.

"NO MATTER HOW MANY TIMES YOU SAVE THE WORLD, IT ALWAYS MANAGES TO GET BACK IN JEOPARDY AGAIN! SOMETIMES I JUST WANT IT TO STAY SAVED, YOU KNOW? FOR A LITTLE BIT. I FEEL LIKE THE MAID: 'I JUST CLEANED UP THIS MESS! CAN WE KEEP IT CLEAN FOR, FOR TEN MINUTES?! PLEASE?!'"

TRAINING TO BE A SUPER

SUPER POWERS AND A SUPERSUIT AREN'T ENOUGH—FIND OUT WHAT IT TAKES TO BECOME THE BEST SUPER YOU CAN BE!

FINDING A MENTOR

MOST SUPERS DON'T START OUT COMPLETELY ON THEIR OWN. FINDING A MENTOR, TRAINER OR EVEN BECOMING A SIDEKICK TO A MORE EXPERIENCED SUPER IS A GREAT WAY TO LEARN THE INS AND OUTS OF SAVING YOUR CITY (OR EVEN THE WORLD!).

IF YOU DON'T ALREADY KNOW A SUPER WHO WILL TRAIN YOU, HERE ARE SOME TIPS FOR FINDING ONE

1. Check the sky for distress signals.

2. Put up flyers, but don't include your contact information—a real Super will be able to find you.

3. Take martial arts or boxing lessons. Even if you don't find a "Super" trainer, you'll still learn a lot of useful skills!

AND IF THE SUPER YOU ASK SAYS NO, DON'T TURN INTO A VILLAIN!

GETTING IN SHAPE

BEING IN TIP-TOP PHYSICAL CONDITION IS IMPERATIVE WHEN YOU'RE A SUPER! EVEN IF YOU'RE ALREADY SUPER STRONG, THERE'S ALWAYS ANOTHER SKILL YOU CAN TRAIN— LIKE GETTING FASTER OR IMPROVING YOUR ENDURANCE, OR EVEN TRAINING YOUR BRAIN.

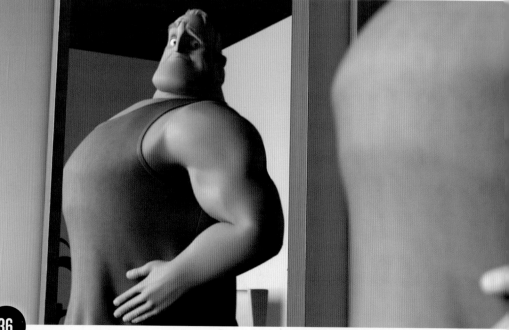

1

One of the best ways you can get in shape is to practice with other Supers-in-training. Make it a competition to see who can jump the highest, run the fastest, swim the farthest or do the most jumping jacks!

2

Another way to work out is to join a sports team! Sports are a great way to get lots of exercise and learn to work as part of a team, which will come in handy when you need to work with other Supers to take down a bad guy.

EVEN SUPERS NEED LOTS OF EXERCISE!

HONING YOUR SKILL

JUST BECAUSE YOU HAVE A SUPER POWER, IT DOESN'T MEAN YOU'RE AUTOMATICALLY GOOD AT USING IT. YOU THINK FROZONE ALWAYS THREW ICE EXACTLY WHERE HE MEANT TO? THINK AGAIN! HE HAD TO WORK ON HIS AIM.

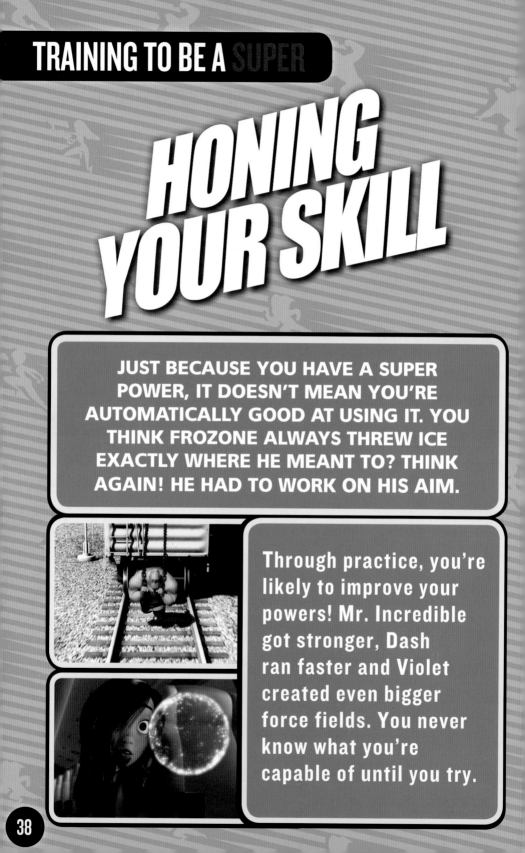

Through practice, you're likely to improve your powers! Mr. Incredible got stronger, Dash ran faster and Violet created even bigger force fields. You never know what you're capable of until you try.

Come up with different ways to practice or enhance your powers—for example, if you can go invisible, then you can practice being super silent. Or if your power requires great aim, like Frozone's, you can practice throwing balls at a target.

EVEN WHEN YOU'RE ALREADY A SUPER, YOU CAN ALWAYS BECOME EVEN MORE AMAZING!

MAKING THE RIGHT CALL

THE SUPER WHO FINISHES A MISSION UNHARMED ISN'T ALWAYS THE FASTEST OR STRONGEST, BUT IS USUALLY THE SMARTEST. THE WAY YOU APPROACH A SITUATION IS JUST AS IMPORTANT AS YOUR SUPER SKILLS—THAT'S WHY IT'S ALWAYS BETTER TO HAVE A PLAN THAN TO JUST RUSH IN AND HOPE FOR THE BEST.

IT PAYS TO BE PREPARED!

1

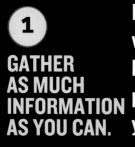

GATHER AS MUCH INFORMATION AS YOU CAN.

Knowing exactly what you need to do and where you need to be for a mission will help you get in—and out!—as quickly as possible. If you need to go somewhere you're unfamiliar with, research it! Look at maps and ask other Supers if they know the area.

2

DETERMINE HOW MANY VILLAINS THERE ARE— AND WHERE THEY ARE.

Knowing how many villains you'll need to get around is crucial. Finding out where they'll be stationed will help you determine which routes you should take and, if you need to face them, whether you should call in reinforcements (i.e., your team of Supers).

3

DISCUSS THE PLAN WITH YOUR SUPER TEAM.

One of the best parts of having a Super team is knowing they'll have your back— and the more Supers planning a mission, the more likely you are to pull it off! If you make a plan that utilizes each Super's special abilities, you'll have the best possible chance of succeeding in your mission.

CREATING A SUPER TEAM

ALL THE BEST SUPERS KNOW IT'S FOOLISH, DANGEROUS AND A LOT LESS FUN TO FIGHT CRIME ON YOUR OWN—THAT'S WHY YOU NEED TO BE PART OF A SUPER TEAM.

DEFINING YOUR TEAM'S MISSION

SO YOU'VE DECIDED THE BEST WAY TO DEFEAT VILLAINS IS TO DO IT AS PART OF A SUPER TEAM? GREAT!

The first step to creating a Super team is deciding what your goals are. Of course you'll be fighting villains, but what specifically do you want to accomplish?

Some Supers are looking to protect their own city from dastardly villains. Some are determined to make the entire world a safer place, while others have decided to protect the environment or be an advocate for animals.

Once you've determined your mission, it will help you find like-minded Supers who want to accomplish the same things you do!

CREATING A TEAM NAME

Having a collective name for your Super team is great for a few reasons. It fosters a sense of unity, you can use it for a team logo and, most importantly, when villains see you all coming they'll say "Curses! It's (team name)!" Trust us—there's nothing better than hearing that!

Your team name could be a superlative, like The Incredibles, or it could tie into your mission—for example, if you're a group of Supers who are also trying to help keep the environment clean, you could call yourselves "The Planet Preservers!"

ONCE YOU HAVE DECIDED
ON A TEAM NAME,
WRITE IT ON THE LINE BELOW

_____

ONE DAY YOU MIGHT BE AS FAMOUS AS "THE INCREDIBLES!"

FINDING OTHER SUPERS

SOMETIMES, THE HARDEST PART OF CREATING A SUPER TEAM IS ACTUALLY FINDING OTHER SUPERS! BECAUSE SUPERS GENERALLY TRY TO STAY UNDERCOVER AND PROTECT THEIR IDENTITY, IT CAN BE DIFFICULT TO GET ONE ON THEIR OWN, SO YOU'LL HAVE TO THINK OUTSIDE THE BOX. HERE ARE A FEW TIPS TO GET YOU STARTED.

1

Use your connections. Did you find a Super to be your mentor back when you were training? Great! Ask him or her if they know of any Supers who are looking for a new team member, or who would be interested in joining a new Super team. Who knows—maybe your mentor will want to join you!

2

Ask your friends. You might not think your friends are Supers, but they probably don't suspect that you're one, either! It never hurts to ask— and if any of them are Supers, you know that you already get along.

3

Join a school sport. Notice any other students who play just a bit better than everyone else? They might be a Super!

OR LOOK FOR KIDS WHO REALLY WANT TO PLAY, BUT AREN'T ALLOWED BECAUSE THEY'LL "SHOW OFF."

FAMILY FIRST

WHEN LOOKING FOR OTHER SUPERS TO JOIN YOUR TEAM, YOU SHOULD ALSO CONSIDER YOUR FAMILY. EVERY FAMILY IS ALREADY PRETTY SUPER IN ITS OWN WAY. YOU KNOW YOU CAN COUNT ON EACH OTHER TO BE THERE WHEN IT MATTERS MOST, YOU ALL KNOW EACH OTHER EXTREMELY WELL AND YOU HAVE A LOT OF PRACTICE WORKING TOGETHER. PLUS, IF YOU WERE BORN WITH SUPER ABILITIES, THERE'S A GOOD CHANCE YOUR FAMILY MEMBERS WILL HAVE THEM TOO!

THERE ARE EVEN MORE PERKS TO BEING A SUPER TEAM WITH YOUR FAMILY:

JUST REMEMBER YOU'LL BE RELYING ON YOUR ANNOYING BROTHER OR SISTER! BUT IT CAN BE KIND OF NICE SOMETIMES.

You won't need to hide your real identity around your family.

You probably already see each other a lot, which makes meeting to plan Super missions a cinch!

You know you can trust your family— no background check required!

SELECTION CRITERIA

NOW THAT YOU HAVE A POOL OF APPLICANTS FOR YOUR SUPER TEAM, YOU CAN DECIDE IF THEY MERIT AN INVITATION!

First, consider their powers. An ideal Super team will consist of a diverse group with different skills, so you each can be useful in different situations. Having five Supers who can run extremely fast would still be cool, but probably not as handy as having one who flies, one who is super fast, one who has telekinesis, one who makes force fields and one who is super strong.

You'll also want to think about whether the Supers you're considering working with are all people who you can rely on. If you're not sure, consider going on a few low-stakes practice missions together.

The Incredibles are a great example of this—when they put all their powers together, they can defeat just about anything!

BELOW, LIST THE SUPERS WHO YOU THINK WOULD WORK WELL ON YOUR TEAM.

TRAINING TOGETHER

ONCE YOU'VE ASSEMBLED YOUR SUPER TEAM, IT'S TIME TO LEARN HOW TO WORK TOGETHER! BEFORE YOU RUN OFF TO FIGHT VILLAINS, DO A FEW OF THESE EXERCISES TO FINE-TUNE YOUR TRUST, COMMUNICATION AND TEAMWORK SKILLS.

1

HERO HULA-HOOP

This sounds silly, but it's harder than it looks! Stand in a close circle with the rest of your Super team, facing inward. Each Super should hold up their hands and extend their index fingers. Have a friend rest a hula hoop on your index fingers. Using just the tips of your index fingers, lower the hula hoop to the ground. Don't hook your finger around the hoop—that's cheating! To make this challenge harder, you can institute a "no talking" rule while carrying it out.

2 SUPER KNOT

Again, stand together in a close circle, facing inward. Each Super must close their eyes and join hands with another Super. Once everyone's hands are joined, open your eyes. Now, figure out how to untie the knot and make a new circle, without letting go of each other's hands!

3 BLIND TRUST

Grab some things for a makeshift obstacle course: some lawn chairs, a bucket of water, ropes, etc. Take turns being blindfolded and letting the rest of the Super team guide the blindfolded Super through the obstacle course, using only their voices. Rearrange the obstacle course each time so that the blindfolded person doesn't know what to expect! (And ask an adult to keep an eye on your training just in case you're all terrible at giving directions.)

THERE'S NOTHING MORE IMPORTANT THAN WORKING TOGETHER. AND PROTECTING YOUR IDENTITY. AND COMING HOME SAFE.

MEET ELASTIGIRL

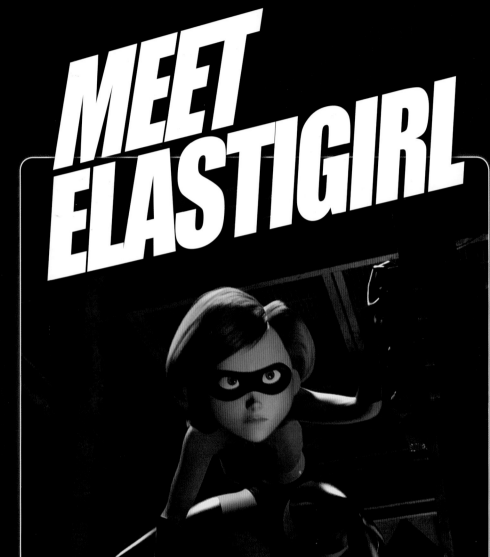

STRENGTH
ENDURANCE
INTELLIGENCE
AGILITY
INDESTRUCTIBILITY

NAME: HELEN PARR

POWERS	FULL BODY ELASTICITY
HEIGHT	5'5.5"
HAIR	BRUNETTE
AGE	LATE 30s
WEIGHT	145 LBS
SUPERSUIT DESIGNER	EDNA MODE
KNOWN ASSOCIATES	MR. INCREDIBLE, FROZONE
CHILDREN	VIOLET, DASH, JACK-JACK
TRIVIA	CAN STRETCH ANY PART OF HER BODY UP TO 100', WITH A MINIMUM THICKNESS OF 1MM.

DID YOU KNOW?

"YOU KNOW IT'S CRAZY, RIGHT? TO HELP MY FAMILY I GOTTA LEAVE IT, TO FIX THE LAW I GOTTA BREAK IT."

- Elastigirl isn't sure how her elasticity works. Her body has always had this amazing ability. But her power isn't limitless—the more she stretches, the more her strength diminishes.

- In her early days, Elastigirl refused to lead a new Super team, "Heroes Incorporated."

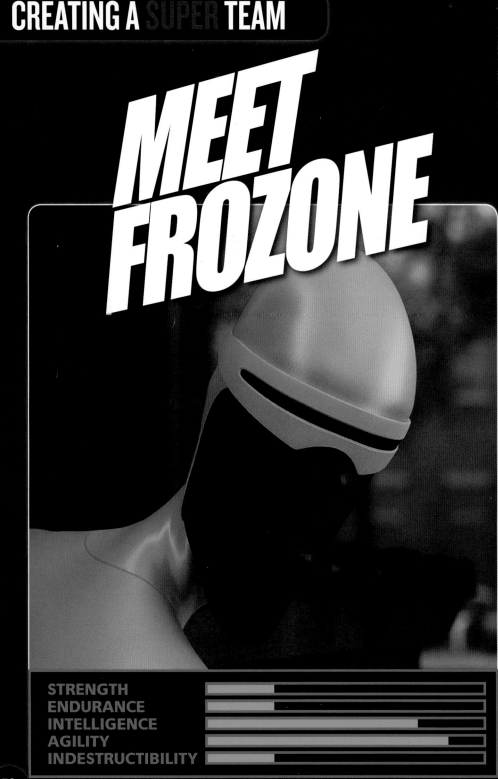

CREATING A SUPER TEAM

MEET FROZONE

STRENGTH
ENDURANCE
INTELLIGENCE
AGILITY
INDESTRUCTIBILITY

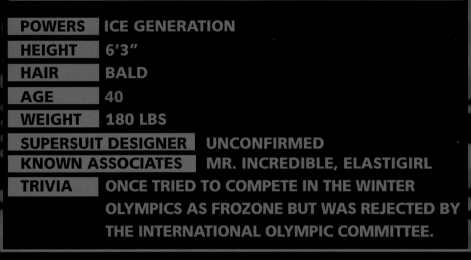

NAME: LUCIUS BEST

POWERS	ICE GENERATION
HEIGHT	6'3"
HAIR	BALD
AGE	40
WEIGHT	180 LBS
SUPERSUIT DESIGNER	UNCONFIRMED
KNOWN ASSOCIATES	MR. INCREDIBLE, ELASTIGIRL
TRIVIA	ONCE TRIED TO COMPETE IN THE WINTER OLYMPICS AS FROZONE BUT WAS REJECTED BY THE INTERNATIONAL OLYMPIC COMMITTEE.

DID YOU KNOW?

"WE ARE TALKING ABOUT THE GREATER GOOD!"

⭐ Frozone's goggles are specially made—they're anti-glare refraction goggles, so he doesn't get snow blindness.

⭐ Frozone's powers are weak in hot and low humidity environments

MEET VOYD

NAME: KAREN FIELDS

POWERS	INTERSPATIAL PORTAL CREATION
HEIGHT	5'5"
HAIR	BLUE
AGE	30s
WEIGHT	130 LBS
SUIT DESIGNER	SELF
KNOWN ASSOCIATES	BRICK, HE-LECTRIX, KRUSHAUER, REFLUX, SCREECH
TRIVIA	BEFORE WORKING TO BECOME A SUPER, VOYD WAS TRIED, BUT NEVER CONVICTED, OF A SERIES OF PETTY THEFTS.

STRENGTH
ENDURANCE
INTELLIGENCE
AGILITY
INDESTRUCTIBILITY

MEET SCREECH

NAME: STRIG TYTON

POWERS AND SPECIALTIES NIGHT VISION, 360°
HEAD ROTATION, SONIC SCREECH, ORNITHOLOGIST,
MECHANICAL ENGINEER

HEIGHT 4'1"

HAIR UNKNOWN

AGE 40s

WEIGHT 80 LBS (DUE TO HOLLOW BONES)

KNOWN ASSOCIATES BRICK, HE-LECTRIX,
KRUSHAUER, REFLUX, VOYD

TRIVIA DEVELOPED AND BUILT HIS FLIGHT SUIT IN
AN AVIARY RESCUE CENTER IN MONTANA.

STRENGTH
ENDURANCE
INTELLIGENCE
AGILITY
INDESTRUCTIBILITY

MEET REFLUX

NAME: GURDLEY MOLA

POWERS	REGURGITATE MOLTEN STOMACH ACID
HEIGHT	4'0"
HAIR	BROWN
AGE	40s
WEIGHT	140 LBS
SUIT DESIGNER	SELF
KNOWN ASSOCIATES	BRICK, HE-LECTRIX, KRUSHAUER, SCREECH, VOYD
TRIVIA	CAMPAIGNED FOR THE SUPER NAME CAPTAIN LAVA BUT SETTLED FOR REFLUX AFTER HE FOUND OUT IT WAS TAKEN.

STRENGTH
ENDURANCE
INTELLIGENCE
AGILITY
INDESTRUCTIBILITY

MEET BRICK

NAME: TARA WALLANDER

POWERS SIZE AND STRENGTH OF A BRICK WALL, SUPER STRENGTH AND ENDURANCE

HEIGHT 7'5"

HAIR RED

AGE 30s

WEIGHT 400 LBS

SUIT DESIGNER SELF

KNOWN ASSOCIATES HE-LECTRIX, KRUSHAUER, REFLUX, SCREECH, VOYD

TRIVIA CAN'T SWIM AND DOESN'T WANT TO.

STRENGTH

ENDURANCE

INTELLIGENCE

AGILITY

INDESTRUCTIBILITY

MEET KRUSHAUER

NAME: BLITZ WAGNER

POWERS	TELEKINETIC CRUSHING AND MANIPULATION
HEIGHT	6'5"
HAIR	BLACK
AGE	30s
WEIGHT	275 LBS
SUIT DESIGNER	SELF
KNOWN ASSOCIATES	BRICK, HE-LECTRIX, REFLUX SCREECH, VOYD
TRIVIA	HOLDS AN OLYMPIC MEDAL FOR LUGE.

STRENGTH
ENDURANCE
INTELLIGENCE
AGILITY
INDESTRUCTIBILITY

MEET HE-LECTRIX

NAME: TOM CURRENT

POWERS CONTROL AND PROJECT ELECTRICITY

HEIGHT 5'10"

HAIR BROWN

AGE 30s

WEIGHT 160 LBS

SUIT DESIGNER SELF

KNOWN ASSOCIATES BRICK, KRUSHAUER, REFLUX, SCREECH, VOYD

TRIVIA HE-LECRIX IS ALSO AN ASPIRING SINGER-SONGWRITER AND GUITARIST FOR A PROG-ROCK COVER BAND.

STRENGTH
ENDURANCE
INTELLIGENCE
AGILITY
INDESTRUCTIBILITY

BRING ON THE BAD GUYS

THIS IS YOUR GUIDE TO EVERY SUPER'S FAVORITE PART OF THE JOB— PROTECTING THE WORLD FROM VILLAINS WHO ARE TRYING TO DESTROY IT!

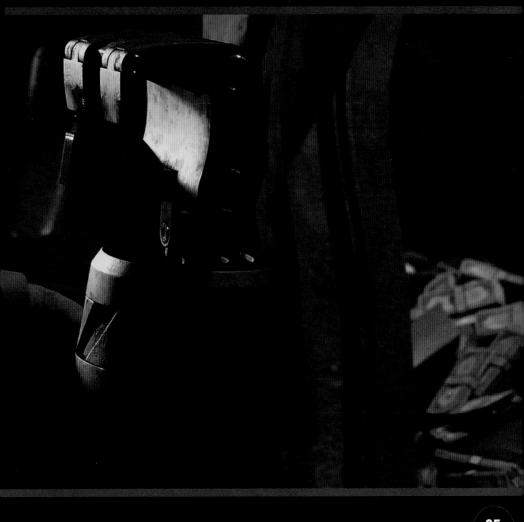

HOW TO SPOT A VILLAIN

HERE'S THE THING: ANYONE CAN BE A VILLAIN. ANYONE! AND IT DOESN'T MATTER HOW THEY'RE DRESSED OR WHAT THEY LOOK LIKE.

Villains are defined by their actions. So keep an eye out for people who are doing things they're not supposed to do, including but not limited to:

1. Robbing banks
2. Explaining elaborate plans
3. Making fun of people
4. Vandalizing buildings
5. Lighting things on fire
6. Laughing maniacally*
7. Pretending to throw balls for dogs
8. Littering
9. Building secret lairs
10. Jaywalking

*NOT ALWAYS VILLAINOUS, BUT DEFINITELY KEEP AN EYE OUT!

HOW TO DETECT A VILLAIN'S WEAKNESS

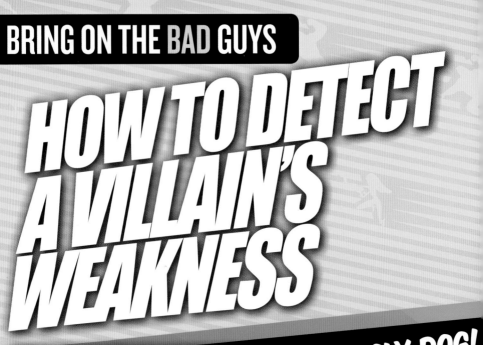

"YOU SLY DOG! YOU HAD ME MONOLOGUING!"

EVERY VILLAIN HAS A WEAKNESS. YOU JUST NEED TO FIND IT! EVEN THE OMNIDROID THAT MR. INCREDIBLE TOOK DOWN COULD BE BEATEN. DESPITE ITS SUPER STRENGTH, HE WAS ABLE TO TRICK THE ROBOT INTO DAMAGING ITSELF. SOME WEAKNESSES ARE EASIER TO SPOT THAN OTHERS. USE THIS GUIDE TO SEE IF THE VILLAIN YOU'RE FACING HAS AN OBVIOUS FLAW.

1. **Does the villain have a cape?** If so, you're in luck! The villain will probably be foiled by his or her own suit without you having to do anything at all. Capes can get tangled up in all sorts of machinery and natural dangers, which is why Edna Mode warns Supers to avoid wearing them.

2. **Is the villain prone to making long speeches or explaining nefarious plans?** Sometimes villains just like to hear themselves talk. When they do, you can use that time to find the flaws in their plans and use the information to stop them before they do anything worse than bore you to tears.

3. **Does the villain have beloved friends or family members who would be disappointed if they knew what was happening?** If so, track down those people (even one will do) and ask them to come to the location where the villain is causing trouble. Oftentimes, villains will give up if they're caught in the act by someone they respect.

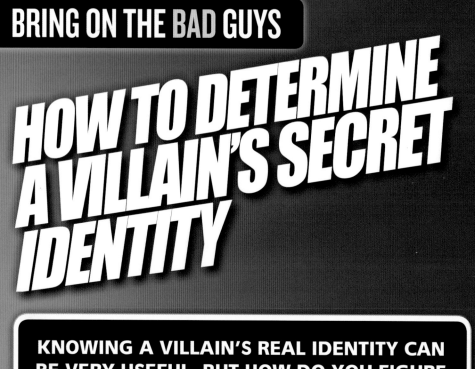

HOW TO DETERMINE A VILLAIN'S SECRET IDENTITY

KNOWING A VILLAIN'S REAL IDENTITY CAN BE VERY USEFUL, BUT HOW DO YOU FIGURE IT OUT? CONSIDER THESE SUGGESTIONS!

Is the villain wearing a full mask? If not, you may be able to recognize who he or she really is based on the rest of his or her facial features.

 Think about who in your town would benefit from the villain succeeding. Is there a wild inventor or mad scientist who would make a lot of money, gain revenge against someone or attain more power if the villain's dastardly plan succeeded? That person might not be the culprit, but they're certainly a lead worth checking out!

3 Think back—if the villain is someone who is targeting you, they might be someone from your own past. Could the villain be someone with whom you've had a previous confrontation?

WHEN TO RETREAT

WE KNOW WHAT YOU'RE THINKING—
SUPERS NEVER GIVE UP, AND THEY
ALWAYS WIN. BUT RETREATING ISN'T
THE SAME AS GIVING UP COMPLETELY.
SOMETIMES YOU NEED TIME TO REGROUP
AND COME UP WITH A PLAN—AND THEN
YOU'LL BE ABLE TO SAVE THE DAY!

If any of these things are happening, you should retreat so you can fight another day:

THERE'S NO SHAME IN REGROUPING!

1. You (or another Super) got hurt.

2. The bad guys are more prepared than you are.

3. You've realized you fell for a trap!

4. You're completely exhausted and out of ideas.

5. It's getting close to your curfew.

MEET THE UNDERMINER

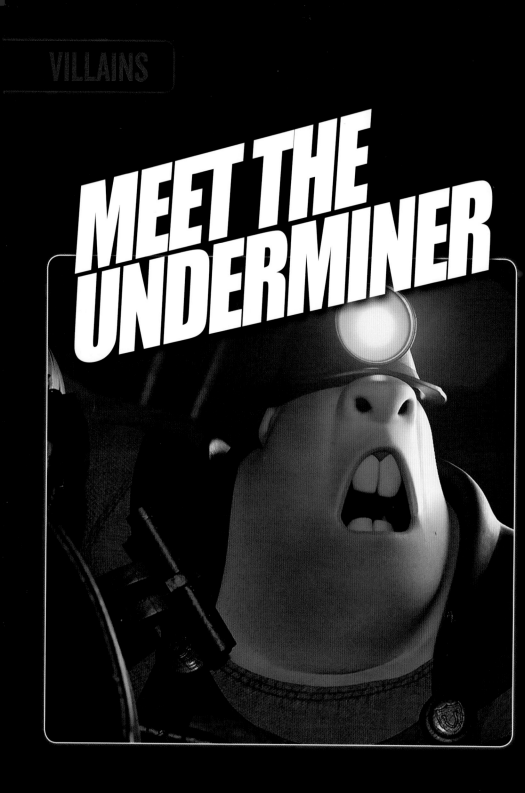

NAME: DOUG TALPID

SPECIALTY	MECHANICAL ENGINEERING, GEOLOGICAL ANARCHIST
WEAPONS	TUNNELER, MECHANICAL GAUNTLETS
HEIGHT	3'6"
HAIR	UNKNOWN
AGE	50s
WEIGHT	175 LBS
KNOWN ASSOCIATES	MOLOIDS, SYNDROME (UNCONFIRMED)
TRIVIA	UNDERMINER'S DRILL BITS ARE MADE FROM A PROPRIETARY ALLOY FROM THE CAVERNS OF NOMANISAN

STRENGTH

ENDURANCE

INTELLIGENCE

AGILITY

INDESTRUCTIBILITY

MEET SYNDROME

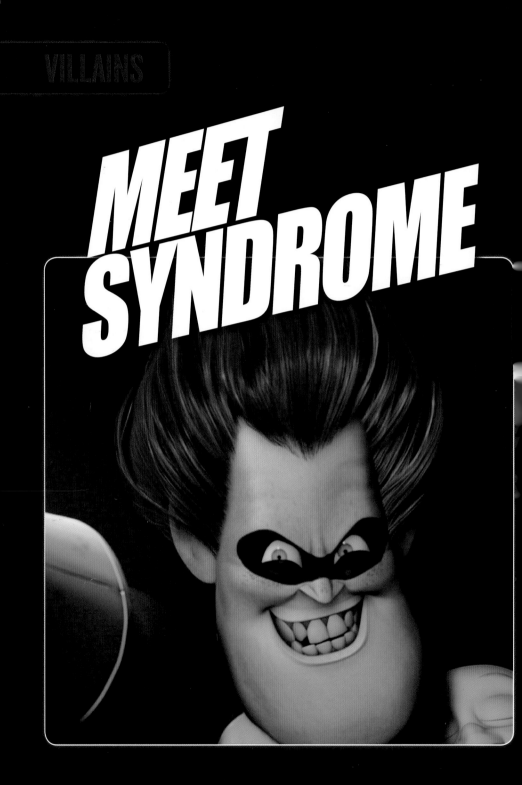

NAME: BUDDY PINE

SPECIALTY INDUSTRIALIST, INVENTOR AND MASTER
ENGINEER

WEAPONS UTILITY GAUNTLETS, AERO BOOTS,
BIO-PROBE, MINIATURE I-BOMB, ZERO POINT
ENERGY

HEIGHT 6'1"

HAIR RED

AGE MID-20S

WEIGHT 185 LBS

SUIT DESIGNER SELF

KNOWN ASSOCIATES MIRAGE (FORMERLY)

TRIVIA THE FIRST AND ONLY INCREDIBOY, BUDDY
WAS MR. INCREDIBLE'S BIGGEST FAN. HIS
FIRST INVENTION WAS THE ROCKET BOOTS.

STRENGTH

ENDURANCE

INTELLIGENCE

AGILITY

INDESTRUCTIBILITY

MEET BOMB VOYAGE

NAME: REMY BON MOT

SPECIALTY DEMOLITIONS AND EXPLOSIVES EXPERT, SOMMELIER

WEAPONS GRENADES, BOMBS

HEIGHT: 6'6"

HAIR BLACK

AGE MID-30s

WEIGHT: 160 LBS

KNOWN ASSOCIATES NONE

TRIVIA WHEN NOT THROWING BOMBS, BOMB VOYAGE MAKES MONEY ON THE STREETS OF FRANCE AS A MIME.

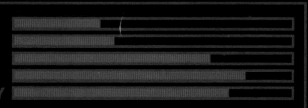

STRENGTH

ENDURANCE

INTELLIGENCE

AGILITY

INDESTRUCTIBILITY

MEET SCREENSLAVER

NAME: EVELYN DEAVOR

SPECIALTY	LEAD DESIGNER OF DEVTECH, JET PILOT, HYPNOMANIPULATION
WEAPONS	HYPNOTIC GOGGLES, HYPNOTECH AND OPTICS
HEIGHT	5'9"
HAIR	BROWN
AGE	40S
WEIGHT:	135 LBS
KNOWN ASSOCIATES	NONE
TRIVIA	DURING HER COLLEGE YEARS, EVELYN CURATED A SERIES OF UNDERGROUND ART SHOWS IN THE BOHEMIAN DISTRICT OF NEW URBEM.

STRENGTH

ENDURANCE

INTELLIGENCE

AGILITY

INDESTRUCTIBILITY

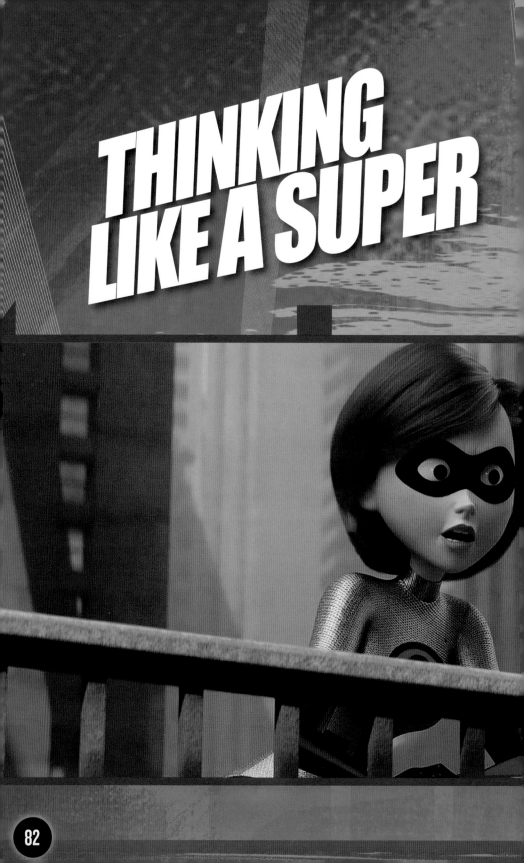

THINKING LIKE A SUPER

AS A SUPER, YOU CAN DO INCREDIBLE THINGS—AND YOU SHOULD LEARN HOW TO WIELD THAT POWER WISELY.

PROTECT YOUR SECRET IDENTITY

AS MR. INCREDIBLE HAS EXPLAINED, "EVERY SUPER HERO HAS A SECRET IDENTITY. I DON'T KNOW A SINGLE ONE WHO DOESN'T. WHO WANTS THE PRESSURE OF BEING SUPER ALL THE TIME?"

NOT ONLY IS IT A LOT OF PRESSURE TO BE A SUPER AT ALL TIMES, IT'S DANGEROUS. GIVING AWAY YOUR SECRET IDENTITY ESSENTIALLY AMOUNTS TO TELLING EVERYONE WHERE YOU LIVE AND WHO YOUR FAMILY IS, AND THAT'S INFORMATION YOU DON'T WANT VILLAINS TO HAVE!

SO, ALWAYS TAKE THE FOLLOWING PRECAUTIONS:

1. Wear your mask while on the job— no exceptions!

2. Resist using your powers in public when you're not in your suit, especially when it's not an emergency.

3. Only wear your Supersuit while you're fighting crime—keep your Super life and your regular life separate.

4. Consider using a different voice when you're in "Super" mode.

5. Don't let being a Super keep you from your regular schedule. If you're always missing school or work, people will get suspicious.

"YOUR SECRET IDENTITY IS YOUR MOST VALUABLE POSSESSION. PROTECT IT."
—ELASTIGIRL

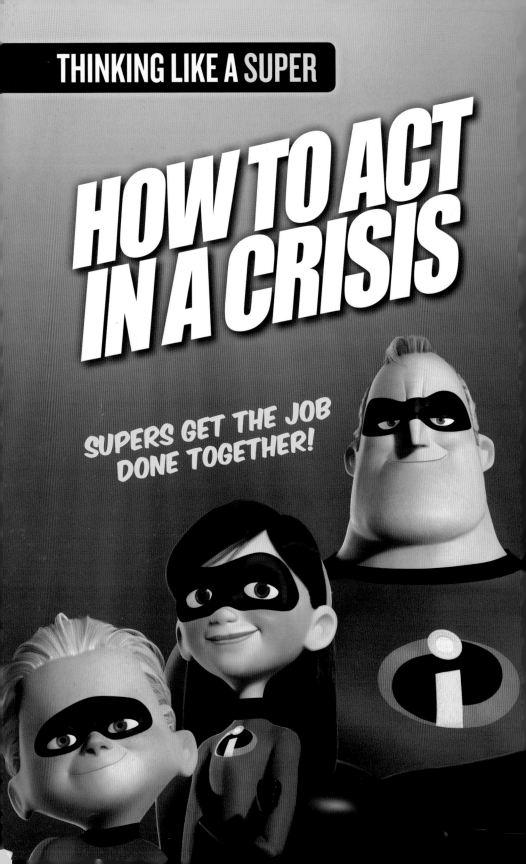

IF YOU FIND YOURSELF STARTING TO LOSE YOUR COOL, FOLLOW THESE TIPS SO YOU CAN STILL SAVE THE DAY!

1. **SLOW DOWN.** We know—being a Super is all about being fast and taking action. But during a crisis, analyze what's happening around you so you can react wisely.

2. **BE POSITIVE.** You're more likely to succeed if you tell yourself that you can do it!

3. **BE HEALTHY.** You're less likely to stress out if you've been taking care of your body. Being in top physical condition (see page 36) and eating right will go a long way in helping you feel prepared to do your Super duty!

4. **CALL FOR BACKUP.** If there's a crisis, you shouldn't have to save the day all by yourself—that's why you have a Super team!

AVOIDING MASS DESTRUCTION

YOUR **NUMBER ONE PRIORITY** WHEN DEALING WITH AN ADVERSARY SHOULD BE TO **AVOID MASS DESTRUCTION** TO THE BEST OF YOUR ABILITY! (PEOPLE ARE A LOT LESS THANKFUL WHEN YOU MAKE A BIG MESS WHILE SAVING THE WORLD.)

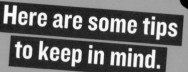

Here are some tips to keep in mind.

1 Try to restrain the criminal as quickly as possible. The less time you spend fighting a villain, the less likely you are to damage nearby areas.

2 Don't destroy cars, trees, statues, etc., unless absolutely necessary.

3 If being chased by villains, lead them away from heavily populated areas.

SUPER QUIZ

IT'S TIME TO PUT ALL YOUR NEWFOUND KNOWLEDGE TO THE TEST.
DO YOU HAVE WHAT IT TAKES TO BE A SUPER?
TAKE THIS QUIZ TO FIND OUT!

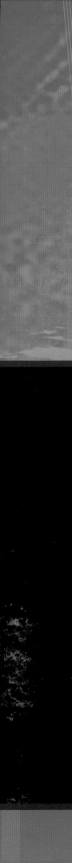

1. What is your most valuable posession?

A. Your powers   C. Your identity

B. Your morals   D. Your Supersuit

2. True or False: Supers don't need to bother training, because they are already super.

ANSWER _____

3. Who can you always depend on?

A. Your coworkers

B. Your family

C. Your bus driver

D. Strangers

4. You and the rest of your Super team are trying to take down a group of villains, but you're outnumbered and one of your teammates has been injured. Do you retreat?

A. Yes

B. Never

C. Not if I can win anyway

Turn the page to continue!

5. What should you consider when picking someone to be on your Super team?

A. Whether their power complements yours

B. Whether or not they are trustworthy

C. How cool their Supersuit looks

D. A and B

6. What is the most important rule when designing your Supersuit?

A. It can't be glittery

B. It must be spandex

C. No capes!!!

D. It should come with a utility belt

ANSWER KEY
TURN THE PAGE UPSIDE DOWN TO SEE ALL THE ANSWERS! YOU EARN ONE POINT FOR EACH CORRECT ANSWER.

1) C; 2) False; 3) B; 4) A; 5) D; 6) C

If you got 1-2 right, you definitely need to reread your *Official Handbook for Young Supers!*

If you got 3-4 right, that's not too bad, but you're not quite ready to be a Super! You should probably study some more.

If you got 5 right, you're so close! But it takes a perfect score to become a Super.

If you got 6 right, **CONGRATULATIONS!** Turn the page to get your graduation certificate!

Media Lab Books
For inquiries, call 646-838-6637

Copyright 2018 Topix Media Lab

Published by Topix Media Lab
14 Wall Street, Suite 4B
New York, NY 10005

Printed in China

ISBN-13: 978-0-9987898-1-1
ISBN-10: 0-9987898-1-X

1CF181

Disney · PIXAR

THE INCREDIBLES
Official SUPER CERTIFICATION

NAME

HAS SATISFACTORILY COMPLETED THE REQUIRED COURSE OF STUDY AND TRAINING TO BECOME A SUPER.

DATE

"YOU HAVE MORE POWER THAN YOU REALIZE."
—ELASTIGIRL